No Job Is Too Big for Frannie B. Miller

FRANKLY, FRANNIE

Rocking Out!

by AJ Stern

illustrated by Doreen Mulryan Marts

Grosset & Dunlap
An Imprint of Penguin Group (USA) Inc.

For Maisie O. Baronian,
who is a rock star in my eyes.—AJS

Thanks as always to everyone at Penguin: Francesco Sedita, Bonnie Bader,
Scottie Bowditch, my editor, Jordan Hamessley, and also, of course,
to Doreen Mulryan Marts, who draws Frannie just like I'd pictured her.
Your support and enthusiasm is unparalleled! To Julie Barer, who
negotiates like nobody's business and to my family and friends for support.
And of course to my nieces and nephews: Maisie, Mia, Lili, Adam,
and Nathan, without whom I'd have lost touch long ago with the
bane and beauty of kid linguistics.—AJS

GROSSET & DUNLAP
Published by the Penguin Group
Penguin Group (USA) Inc., 375 Hudson Street, New York, New York 10014, USA
Penguin Group (Canada), 90 Eglinton Avenue East, Suite 700, Toronto, Ontario M4P 2Y3,
Canada (a division of Pearson Penguin Canada Inc.)
Penguin Books Ltd., 80 Strand, London WC2R 0RL, England
Penguin Group Ireland, 25 St. Stephen's Green, Dublin 2, Ireland
(a division of Penguin Books Ltd.)
Penguin Group (Australia), 250 Camberwell Road, Camberwell, Victoria 3124, Australia
(a division of Pearson Australia Group Pty. Ltd.)
Penguin Books India Pvt. Ltd., 11 Community Centre,
Panchsheel Park, New Delhi—110 017, India
Penguin Group (NZ), 67 Apollo Drive, Rosedale, Auckland 0632, New Zealand
(a division of Pearson New Zealand Ltd.)
Penguin Books (South Africa) (Pty.) Ltd., 24 Sturdee Avenue,
Rosebank, Johannesburg 2196, South Africa

Penguin Books Ltd., Registered Offices: 80 Strand, London WC2R 0RL, England

Text copyright © 2012 by AJ Stern. Illustrations copyright © 2012
by Penguin Group (USA) Inc. All rights reserved. Published by Grosset & Dunlap,
a division of Penguin Young Readers Group, 345 Hudson Street, New York, New York 10014.
GROSSET & DUNLAP is a trademark of Penguin Group (USA) Inc. Printed in the U.S.A.

Library of Congress Control Number: 2011046445

ISBN 978-0-448-45750-5 (pbk)   10 9 8 7 6 5 4 3 2 1
ISBN 978-0-448-45751-2 (hc)   10 9 8 7 6 5 4 3 2 1

ALWAYS LEARNING   **PEARSON**

CHAPTER

Every day something happens in Chester, New York. A for instance of what I mean is just yesterday we found out that our neighbors, the Demirs, are moving back to Istanbul. That's where they're from. **It's a scientific fact** that Istanbul is in a place called Turkey, and that is not an opinion. That was really sad news.

And today, my teacher, Mrs. Pellington, told us some news that became the second bad news of the week. The recreation center across the street from school might shut down! Noah Zark came to Chester, New York, six months ago and opened up a recreation center called Noah's Ark. If you say *Noah Zark* out loud, it sounds like *Noah's Ark*. Isn't that **fantastical**? I would love for my name to do something twice like that. But it just says *Frannie Miller. Frankly* when I'm working. *Mrs. Frankly B. Miller* on envelopes.

Noah's Ark is the most **amazingish** place where all the town kids go after school. It's only been alive for a very short time, but it's very, very popular. That doesn't always happen for new places. **However and nevertheless**, even though they are very popular, they still haven't made enough money. The very **seriousal** part is that if they don't make enough money to pay their rent next month, they will have to close down forever!

Everyone loves Noah's Ark. Even adults. They have café tables and coffee, which are two things adults really love. There is ice cream, too, and Noah names the flavors after kids who do something amazingish. If you get on the honor roll or score a big goal or get an A plus, like that. I don't have an ice-cream flavor named for me yet. There is a theater where kids put on plays and comfy couches where the older kids can do their homework. You can dress up using the big costume box or draw a **millionty** pictures using their **foreverteen** amount of art supplies.

And on rainy days on the weekend, and sometimes even after school, they show movies! Everybody wanted to save the Ark. That is why all the adults had a meeting to come up with just how to do that.

Tonight, my babysitter, Tenley, who is also my best friend Elliott's babysitter, let Elliott and me stand by the front door to wait for my parents to come home after the meeting. Elliott was going to eat dinner with us when my parents got home.

Elliott and I stared out the front window. I could not wait to hear about all the geniusal ideas they came up with to save the Ark. I kept thinking I heard my parents, but each time it was actually the Demirs getting ready to have a big sale over the weekend. Since they were moving to Turkey, they had to sell a lot of their things. So they were planning to have a sale outside their house.

I liked the Demirs, and I was very sad they were leaving. Especially because they have a very big dog named Winston Churchill who I love to play with. My parents don't think I'm responsible enough for a pet, so sometimes I pretend Winston Churchill is mine. Just when I thought I heard the Demirs again, I saw headlights, and Elliott and I realized that this time it was actually my parents!

I was jumping up and down waiting for them to get inside. Elliott was bouncing a little bit, but not **full jumping**. The second the door opened, I started to ask them very important questions.

"Well? Did anyone come up with good ideas? What were the ideas? Anything geniusal?"

They smiled and my mom kissed me.

"Hi, love," she said to my head top. "Hi, Elliott," she said, rustling his hair with one hand and handing my dad her coat with the other.

"Hi, Mrs. Miller," Elliott said.

"Let us get a little settled, Birdy," my dad said, walking to the coat closet. My dad is the only person who calls me Birdy. Bird is my middle name. (Elliott knows, but please don't tell anyone else about that fact.)

"Tenley, we're home!" my mother called. Tenley came out of the living room.

When my mom went to the kitchen,

I followed her, and Elliott followed me. Then my dad came in, and Tenley followed him! My mom put on the kettle for tea. Everyone except me sat down at the kitchen table. My legs were too **excitified** to do any **knee-bending**.

"I am too suspensified!" I said, jumping in the air just once. "If I don't find out what happened at the meeting, my skin is going to fall off!"

"Well, everyone had very good ideas," my mom said. "But it was your father who had the best idea!"

I looked at my dad with the biggest **pride-itity** in my eyes. "What was your idea?" I asked him.

"A rock concert. We'll have a famous musician play a concert at the Ark and raise money to save it."

"That is the most geniusal idea that

my brain has ever heard," I told him as I went over and sat on his **geniusal** lap.

"Who's going to give the concert?" Elliott asked.

"That's just the thing," my dad said. "We don't know any famous musicians!"

I was **stumpified**. I looked at Tenley, but she shrugged and made her "I don't know any famous musicians, either" face.

"It's officially a contest," my mom explained, sitting down at the table with us with her hot tea.

"What do you mean?" Tenley asked.

"Everyone can propose an idea, and if Noah picks your idea, then you'll get an ice-cream flavor named after you."

That was my **absolute life dream**. I knew right then that I had to make the best musician suggestion possible, otherwise I would *never* get a flavor named after me.

"What if he doesn't like *any* of the ideas?" I asked, getting a little worrified.

"He has that all worked out," my dad started to explain. "He's friends with some of the local bands, and they said they'd be happy to play if he couldn't find a rock star."

"Can Elliott and I be excused, please?" I asked.

Elliott looked at me, confused.

"We have to hold a very important meeting in my office," I told my parents.

CHAPTER

Elliott raced after me as I ran to my bedroom, which was also my office. When we got there, Elliott still looked **confusified**.

"We have to think of the musician, Elliott. We have to win the contest and get flavors named after us."

That's when Elliott immediately lay down on my bed and stared at the ceiling. This is how he does his best thinking. I paced back and forth because sometimes when I distractify my brain, it comes up with some of its best ideas.

Elliott sat up quickly. "Who is Eliza Doolittle again?" he asked.

"She was in the movie *My Fair Lady*," I told him.

"Oh," he said, and flopped back

down on his back. I paced. Elliott
flung himself back up. "The Von Trapp
family—wait! Never mind, they're not
real, either." He went back down to
think again. "Violet Beauregarde!" he
called, jumping back up.

"She's from *Charlie and the
Chocolate Factory*," I reminded him.
"And she's not a musician!"

"I don't think I'm very good at this," Elliott said.

That was true, actually. I wasn't much better, though, because I couldn't even think of one singer. Sometimes when you *really have* to get your brain together, it dries out and there is nothing there. It is very **frusterizing**.

"Dinner!" my mom called. That put an end to our very important meeting. I raced down to dinner and Elliott raced after me.

"Billy Elliot!" he called behind me.

"From a musical!" I yelled back.

Elliott loved to eat dinner at my house. He loved it because both my parents were very good cooks, so no matter who made dinner, Elliott knew it would be very delicious. Elliott's parents are divorced. Even though his dad lives down the block from Elliott, it was still very sad. However and nevertheless, Elliott's mom had a new boyfriend named George. He was a friend of my dad's, actually. George wasn't at Elliott's house tonight, and Elliott's mom was the most **terriblist** cook. So Elliott chose us.

After we raised our glasses and clicked them together and said, "To the Millers!" Elliott and I admitted that we didn't come up with anything good in our meeting. Which made my parents think about the musicians they loved from the olden days. The bands they loved had the **weirdiest** names ever. One band my dad liked was called Talking Heads. Another was named the Goo Goo Dolls, and my mom loved a band called the Squirrel Nut Zippers.

When she said that, Elliott and I almost toppled out of our chairs, we were laughing so hard. Just when we stopped laughing, I thought of something. I didn't mean to interrupt, but sometimes my mouth has a brain of its own.

"Aimee Chapman!" I blurted out.

My parents and Elliott stopped talking. They all looked at me.

"Aimee Chapman," my dad said, like it was a statement type of sentence.

"Aimee Chapman," my mom said in a "that is the most geniusal idea I've ever heard in my worldwide life" voice.

"Aimee Chapman," Elliott said in his "I cannot believe that my best friend is the smartest person who was ever born on this planet" voice.

Aimee Chapman is a very famous singer who even has songs in movies.

She is a grown-up type of singer, but she is **funnish**, so everyone loves her, kids and adults. She wears stylish clothes, like swirly colored scarves and hats with feathers in them and blazers that are too big for her. They make her look sometimes like she is going to an office. That is one of my favorite parts about her, outside of her songs, which I really love and know all the words to. I've seen pictures of her, and she even carries her guitar in a guitar type of briefcase. That makes me feel like we would be very good friends and be **understandable** of each other.

Aimee Chapman was the right person for the job of saving Noah's Ark. We all felt that way. That was why after dinner, my parents, Elliott, and I jumped into the car and drove over to the Ark to tell Noah. We all ran to the front door and knocked.

"Come on, Noah!" I said out loud. "Please be inside."

We knocked again.

When we were convinced he'd gone home for the day, we headed back to the car and, just then, Noah opened the door!

"Noah!" I called.

Elliott and I ran back to the door and my parents followed us.

"What's going on?" he asked.

That's when I looked at him, and in my most **seriousal** and professional

voice of ever I said, "Aimee Chapman."

Then he broke out into a very handsome smile, nodded his head, and said her name.

"Aimee Chapman," he said in his most official "you have won this contest. There will be a very special flavor of ice cream named after you" voice.

CHAPTER

Noah's Ark was going to get much more **excitifying**. Everyone heard the news that Aimee Chapman was the person who Noah was going to ask to play the concert. I felt the biggest **pride-itity** of ever inside myself. The day after I said the words *Aimee Chapman* to Noah, my friends and I ran to the Ark after school to see if she'd said yes yet.

"We *just* asked her this morning!"

Noah told us, laughing. "We probably won't hear until the end of the week," he said.

Millicent, Elliott, Elizabeth, and I all looked at one another with "until the end of the week?????" eyeballs. We could not wait that long. That is when I got an honestly **geniusal** idea. I motioned for everyone to follow me downstairs.

While they sat down at a table, I ran to get colored pens and paper.

"We're all going to write Aimee Chapman letters! Everyone loves to get letters! Everyone loves to open letters!" I was practically singing, I was so excitified. "We'll write her letters to convincify her to play here. We'll tell her how much we love her and how much we love the Ark. She can't say no. Not to letters!" I cried.

Millicent, Elizabeth, and Elliott agreed that it was a geniusal idea.

It took a long time to come up with the exact right things to say, but finally we were all writing really fast and a lot. So much that Elizabeth needed more paper. Elliott drew a picture of the stage with Aimee Chapman singing on it, and Millicent wrote her letter as a story. My letter was very simple, and it went like this:

Dear Mrs. Aimee (I do not
know your middle name)
Chapman,

It is a scientific fact that
you are everyone's favorite
musician. That is why you are
the only one who can save
the world in Chester, New
York. Our grown-up friend
Noah owns Noah's Ark, which
is a place where all the kids
can go. Adults can come,
too, of course. Without the
Ark, some kids would go home
and be all by themselves
until their parents came
home from work. When they
go to Noah's Ark, they have
company! It's also really good
because they let you make
art and music there.

However and nevertheless,
if they don't make enough

money in just a couple weeks,
they have to close down.
FOREVER. The only way to
save noah's Ark is to do
something very amazingish
and special. This is a for
instance of why we want
you to play a concert. Please,
Mrs. Aimee (I do not know
your middle name) Chapman,
help us save the Ark.

Your friend-to-be,
Frannie B. Miller

P.S. You can call me
Frankly because that is my
professional name. It even
says so on my résumé (that's
a list of all the places I've
worked).

When we were done with our
letters, we went to the office and

presented them to Noah. He was very **impresstified**. Noah gave us all envelopes and we wrote Aimee's manager's address on them. He let us put the stamps on and said he would be sure to send them. I had a very good day feeling on my skin about this. But before we left, I got a little bit of a **worry tickle** in my brain.

"Noah?" I asked him.

"Hmmm . . . ?" he said, writing something down on a very official sheet of paper. It was so official, it had a name: letterhead. That's where the paper says something on top. In this case, what it said on top was NOAH'S ARK. My letterhead was going to say MRS. FRANKLY B. MILLER, PROFESSIONAL WORKER.

"What if Aimee Chapman says no?"

That's when Noah looked up. "Since the fund-raiser has to go on with or without her, I've asked three local bands to step in if she says no. We'll do a battle of the bands," he said.

I liked the sound of that: battle of the bands. But I wanted Aimee Chapman.

"That sounds good," I told him, although really what sounded good was the name of it. Secretly I hoped that our letters would make her say yes! Elliott, Millicent, Elizabeth, and I left, ran down the stairs, waited for our parents, and then went home to wait some more.

My mom put on an Aimee Chapman CD, while my dad and I helped her fix dinner. Sometimes we have dance parties, but not on purpose. This was one of those times. We are a very **dancey** kind of family. We danced all through making dinner, and then we danced our way to the table. It was very **funnish**. At dinner I told my parents about the letters we wrote, and they said they were a very good idea.

"If Aimee Chapman says yes, it will all be because of you, Birdy."

I felt hot redness blush itself on my cheeks. I didn't want to be **braggish** about it, but I smiled because I agreed with my dad in an inside type of way.

"Aimee Chapman was your idea, and the letters were your idea, too. Quite an accomplishment, kiddo," he told me. My dad always made me so happy with his compliments. That was when I told my parents the big news about the type of new job I wanted to get.

"I have decided to be a person who puts on concerts," I told them. "They have offices, letterhead, stamps, envelopes, and copiers," I explained.

"Do you mean a producer?" my dad asked.

"Is that what Noah is?" I asked.

"Well, he's the owner and director of Noah's Ark, but because he is putting on and organizing a concert, that makes him a producer. A concert producer."

"I want to be a concert producer, too," I told them.

"Well, it sounds like you are well on your way," my mom said. I felt that was true, which was why my smile went from the entire west side of Chester, New York, to the entire east side of Chester, New York.

Later that night after my bath, my parents came in to kiss me good night and tell me **excitifying** news. They said that they just got off the phone with Noah. I sat up really straight and fast.

"Did Aimee Chapman say she'd do the concert?" I asked.

"No, he hasn't heard anything yet," my dad said. "However, Noah mentioned that he needs extra hands."

My mom butted in. "I mentioned that you expressed interest in being a concert producer and said you might be interested in applying for a job. And you will never believe what he said, Frannie." My mom made her eyes very **bigful**.

"What? What?" I couldn't even wait to know.

"He said he was hiring!" my dad finished for her.

"It's a part-time job. It will take place after school. Three days a week for the next two weeks until the concert. So, tomorrow you can go directly to the Ark after school and give Noah your résumé and a business card. I think he might even interview you!"

Interview me? **That was a dream come true.**

"What will I do at this job?" I asked.

"Whatever he needs you to do," my mom said. "Isn't that exciting?"

It was. It was so exciting, I couldn't even speak. I just smiled the biggest smile of ever and nodded my head. It was actually and nevertheless that exciting.

CHAPTER

Before breakfast, I put my résumé and business cards into my briefcase. I also put in my dad's old glasses that didn't have any lenses, his old cell phone, some batteries, a writing pad, pencils, an oversize eraser, and a few folders and permanent markers. I didn't know what kind of tools a concert producer needed, so I packed what I thought I might need.

I could not wait to give Noah

my résumé. He was going to be so **impresstified** with how many jobs I've had. My parents didn't say he would *definitely* interview me, but I hoped that he would, because I had never had an **actual** interview before.

I think it is important to do things you've never done before, except for if it's **dangerous**. Interviews are not dangerous, which is a for instance of why I wanted to have one. It's also a for instance of why I took my résumé out of my briefcase and wrote across the top in pencil, PLEASE INTERVIEW ME FOR A JOB.

Then I went to school.

School took forever and ever and ever and ever and one last ever to be over. At lunch I told Elliott, Millicent, and Elizabeth that I was applying for a job at Noah's Ark. They wanted to apply for one also, but **it's a scientific fact** that I am the only kid in my class with a résumé.

"I will probably need an assistant, though," I told them. "Maybe even three. So you can all work for me!"

"All of us?" Elliott asked. "Three assistants?"

I nodded my head with **pride-itity**.

"But usually you only have one. *Me*," he reminded me.

"You will be my top-level assistant, Elliott," I told him. This gave him a **worldwide smile**, but when I turned to Millicent and Elizabeth, I saw that they were not smiling even one inch.

"We have worked for you before," Millicent said.

"And it wasn't the best experience," Elizabeth added.

"You always get in trouble," Millicent reminded me.

"There is no way I will get in any trouble this time. I am a born concert producer. Just you wait," I informed them in my **concert producer-ish** voice.

"Everyone deserves a second chance," Elliott told them.

"And sometimes even a third and a fourth," I chimed in, just in case this was more than my second chance, **actually**.

They agreed with me, which was why they let themselves be hired.

After school, we ran across the street to Noah's Ark. Before I went inside, though, I had to capture my breath so it didn't boggle around so much. Applying for a job was very **nervousing**.

My three assistants, Elliott, Millicent, and Elizabeth, went inside before me. Outside, I opened my briefcase, pulled out my résumé and business card, and then closed it back up. When I was ready, I walked inside with my chin up and shoulders back, gripping the handle of my briefcase hard in one hand. In my other hand I held my résumé and business card.

I walked right to Noah's office. Even though the door was open, I knocked on it, because that is what a **professional grown-up** who is about to be interviewed for a job would do. Noah looked up and smiled.

"Frannie, come in. I've been expecting you," he said.

I smiled.

"Is that your résumé?" he asked.

I nodded and handed it to him.

He took it and looked it over and then motioned with his chin toward an empty chair.

"Have a seat," he said.

"Are you going to interview me?" I asked, really **excitified**.

"Well, that's what it says here at the top of the résumé."

I sat down and put my briefcase on the ground. Then I put my hands in my lap because I did not know what a person was supposed to do with their hands during an interview.

"Do you have a lot of work experience?" Noah asked.

"Yes, I have a lot, actually. I've been a radio talk show host, a dog veterinarian, a restaurant critic, a fortune-teller, a keynote speaker, and a principal for a day," I said. "Half a day, actually," I corrected myself. That job didn't work out so well. Actually, not very many had worked out so well.

"And what about rock stars? Do you have a lot of experience with them?" he wanted to know.

This question **stumpified** me. I didn't actually have *any* experience

with rock stars. But then I realized
something.

"No, I do not. However and
nevertheless, I am a very fast learner,
and I get along with a lot of grown-ups.
I have never met a rock star grown-up,
but I'm sure that Aimee Chapman and
I will get along because I know all the
words to her songs. And also because
I like her scarves. And because she
carries a guitar briefcase."

"Very well," Noah said. "Are you
willing to work late? Can you work long
hours?" he asked me.

"I can work until I have to go home
for dinner," I told him. "Sometimes
I might have to do some homework,
though, before I start my job."

"Fantastic. Can you make coffee and
pick up the phone on the half ring?"

"I don't know how to make coffee, but my dad can teach me. I will learn how to pick up the phone on the half ring. I will practice at home day and night," I told him.

"Great. You won't have to do those things; I just wanted to know," Noah said with a smirk that showed his face dimples. Then he stood up, held out his arm, and we shook hands.

"Frannie B. Miller—"

"Frankly," I interrupted. "My professional name is Frankly."

"Sorry. Frankly—"

"Mrs.," I cut in again. "Mrs. Frankly B. Miller."

"Mrs. Frankly B. Miller," Noah said. "You are officially hired."

CHAPTER

My heart almost flew out of my chest and hit Noah in the face. I was so happy about this news.

"What should I do first?"

"What would be most helpful to me would be if you picked out the green room," he told me.

"Okay, Noah. I'll do that," I told him, and ran downstairs to Millicent, Elliott, and Elizabeth and told them that I was hired! My first job was to look for a green room. Since they were all my assistants, I asked them to help. We walked down the long hallway and looked for green rooms, but every room we saw was white. None of us remembered ever seeing a green room. We looked around **forty hundred** times, but we were just going in and out of the same rooms. I did not know what to do about this. I didn't want to get fired on my very first day. But if I told Noah that we couldn't pick out a green room because we couldn't find it, he'd think I was bad at my job. Or color-blind!

I was **stumpified**. That is why I decided to hold a meeting. We all sat down at my café table–office and I told them that we needed to discuss what I should do. We decided I should go upstairs and tell Noah that we looked everywhere for the green room, and we are **very certainly** sorry, but we could not find it. Maybe someone accidentally painted it white when no one was looking?

I went back upstairs to the office, very **nervousingly**, and knocked on the door.

"Frankly!" Noah said.

"Noah?" I asked him.

"Yes?"

"Elliott, Millicent, and Elizabeth are working for me as my assistants, and we all looked very hard for it, but we could not find a room that is green. I am very sorry, and I hope that you don't fire me. If you give us paint, we can paint a room green for you!" I offered.

Noah slapped a palm against his forehead and said, "Oh, Frankly! I sometimes forget that you're not an adult. A green room is a special VIP room for performers or people about to take the stage. It's a place for them to relax and be calm and comfy before they appear in public. The green room isn't actually green in color. It's just part of the name. I don't know why it's called the green room. I guess we could look it up."

"So you don't want me to find you a room that is green colored?"

"No, I do not," Noah stated.

"You want me to pick out the comfiest room you have?" I said, just to make sure I was getting everything right.

"Exactly. Think you can do that?"

"Yes, I can," I told him, because that was a scientific fact.

I ran back downstairs to tell the others.

"It's just an expression!" I explained. "It's what they call the room for performers. It's not actually green at all! That's just what they call it!" I told them.

"So how do we pick it?" Elizabeth asked.

"We have to pick the most comfortablish room. That's the job of the green room, to be very comfy."

"Like a bedroom?" Millicent asked.

"I guess," I said. "Bedrooms are very comfortable."

"That's true. They are," Elliott said.

"But so are living rooms!" Millicent chimed in.

"That's true, too," I agreed. This was much more complicated than I thought.

"Our library is very comfortable," Elizabeth said. I've been in her library, and the couches are some of the **smooshiest** I've ever sat on.

"Are we supposed to *make* the room comfy, or is it just supposed to already *be* comfy?" Millicent asked.

They were asking me some very good questions indeed, but nevertheless they were **stumpifying**. I did not want to bother Noah again.

"Both?" I said-asked.

And so that's what we decided we'd do. We'd not only pick out the comfiest room at Noah's Ark, but we'd make it even comfier than it already was! We went back down the hall and into every room again.

The first room was just a place where there were a lot of supplies, and it wasn't that comfortable. A for instance of what I mean is that there was no couch. The second room was a bathroom, so that wouldn't work. The other room was a janitor's closet, and the last two rooms were dressing rooms. But across the hall from the last dressing room was a room whose door was always shut. That's why none of us ever went in there. But I was the boss

of everything, so I opened the door. I
did it slowly, just in case something
really **terrible-ish** happened. But the
opposite of terrible happened. It was a
very comfortable room! And it had two
couches! And a special table with a big
mirror that had lights all around it.
And a small refrigerator. We all looked
at one another with "this is the best
green room of any green room I've ever
seen" eyes.

Once we had it picked out, I ran
upstairs to tell Noah.

"Which one?" he asked.

"The room in the back with the two
couches," I told him.

That's when Noah smiled so hard,
his own head almost fell off.

"That's the exact room I was
thinking we'd use," he said. "You are

really good at this job, Frankly."

That's when I almost bowed, but didn't.

"Now all we need is for Aimee to say yes. And if she does, she'll send a rider and we'll follow the instructions for how to set up the green room," he told me.

I had no idea what any of that meant. But I said okay, anyway.

Then Noah reached his hand out for me to shake. While he was shaking my hand all up and down, he said, "Congratulations, Frankly. Your first day at work is finished. You may go home and have dinner now."

That is when I did actually bow. And he bowed back, and we both laughed because we were feeling so happy about my great green room–picking job.

CHAPTER

When I got home, my dad was just getting back from work. Before he even put his briefcase down, I ran to him.

"I need to learn how to make coffee!" I cried. "I got a job and I don't know how to make coffee!"

"Congratulations, Birdy! That's amazing. If you give me a few minutes to settle in, I will teach you how to make coffee," he said. I followed him around until he was ready. Then we went into the kitchen where we got the coffeemaker.

It had a lot of complicated parts. There was something called a filter. You have to put coffee in there. Then you put water in a hole in the machine. Then you turn it on. I wrote it all down so I wouldn't forget how to make coffee ever.

At dinner, I told my parents all the **excitifying** things that were going on at Noah's Ark. They said that I had the most exciting career of everyone in the entire Miller household.

"Do you know about green rooms and riders?" I asked them.

"We do, indeed," my dad said while my mom nodded her head.

"Does the rider come in on a horse or a bicycle?" I asked them.

They looked at each other **confusified**, like they didn't know what I was talking about.

"What are you talking about, Frannie?" my dad asked.

"A rider. Noah said we had to wait for Aimee Chapman's rider, and then we would follow their instructions. I just want to know when the rider will come so I can be outside at the right time to meet it."

My dad slapped his hand down on the table, laughing. "Oh, Frannie!" he said. "You're too much."

"A rider," my mom started to explain, "is a type of contract. It's a list of requests from a rock star. They ask for things they want in their green room."

"What sort of things?" I asked.

"Things that they really like," my mom said.

"A lot of rock stars ask for special food and chocolate," my dad told me.

"Others ask for candles or towels or tea or candy. It really depends on what kind of person it is. Big rock stars ask for *big* things, and smaller rock stars ask for smaller things. Make sense?"

I nodded my head.

"Some very big rock stars even tell the producers how they want the green room decorated!" my mom said.

"I've changed my mind about something," I told her.

"What's that?" she asked.

"I don't want to be a concert producer anymore."

"You don't?" my dad asked, looking very sad about this news.

"No, I want to be a rock star," I told him. "So I probably need a rider if I'm going to be a rock star," I told them.

"Probably," my dad told me, adding, "I think I should have a rider if I'm going to be a rock star's dad."

"I would like a rider as a rock star's mom!" my mom said. "What's going to go on your rider?" she asked me.

"You'll see," I told her. I didn't tell them what exactly I was going to put because I didn't actually know yet. That is why I ate dinner as **fastly** as possible. I was going to have a long night ahead of me making a rider.

I didn't know whether riders should be on nice paper or not, but I decided they should be. Also the pages should be stapled. Even if the rider wasn't two pages, I was going to put a staple in it. Staples make everything look more **seriousal**. So do paper clips.

I went to my desk, where I keep all my important office supplies, and pulled out a very fancy pen, nice paper, my stapler, a folder with two pockets, and a manila envelope.

Then I sat at my desk and realized something **horrendimous**. Green rooms were not actually offices, and I really only wanted to work in an office. Having a job was only fun if you got to have a real-life office. Then I got a geniusal idea and started to write.

MY ROCK STAR RIDER
by Mrs. Frankly B. Miller

Hello there. This is my rider. A rider is a list of all the things I want in my green room.

1. A very professional-looking desk
2. An assistant
3. A copy machine
4. White, long envelopes and stamps
5. A fax machine
6. A scanner
7. A three-hole punch
8. Lined writing paper
9. A postal scale
10. Filing cabinets
11. Legal pads

I read the list over to myself to see if anything was missing. There were some **officey** things missing, but I thought eleven was a very good amount of things to ask for. If I asked for any more, I would feel like I was being too **asky**.

I brought my rider downstairs to my parents. They read it and laughed and said, "Frannie, you are too much."

I knew they didn't mean that they wished there was less of me. They meant that they think I'm funny. Apparently and nevertheless, not all kids want to have an office and get a job. I brought my rock star rider back to my bedroom office and slipped it into a manila envelope. Before I sealed it, I put my résumé and a business card inside. Then I sealed it. On the front I wrote MRS. FRANKLY B. MILLER'S ROCK STAR RIDER.

I was not exactly sure what I was going to do with it, but I knew I might need it, so I kept it on my desk just in case. Then my parents decided it was time for bed.

CHAPTER

The next morning was a Saturday,
and the Demirs were having a very
big house sale. That meant they were
selling everything inside their house,
not their actual house. Elliott and I
offered to sell lemonade so that people
could have refreshments. We made a
very large pitcher of half lemonade and
half iced tea. My dad helped us set up
our stand, which was a card table with
a tablecloth on top and two stools side

by side. I made a sign that read: STOP
BY THE LEMONADE STAND OFFICE!

Winston Churchill was getting in
the way a little bit, so we made him
our Lemonade Office dog. All he had
to do was keep us company. That was
a really helpful thing for us to do,
apparently and nevertheless.
Mrs. Demir told us.

The Demirs had *a lot* of stuff. They had stuff outside of the house on blankets, on their lawn, and on tables. Plus, they had all the stuff inside the house that they were selling, too. Mrs. Demir was very worried about getting everything sold in time for their move. She didn't know how she was going to do it all. And Winston Churchill— she didn't know what to do about Winston Churchill!

"What do you mean?" I finally asked her when she said it again to my mom.

"I just don't know if we can take the dog. It's too much. I mean, maybe we could send for him later, but I'm not sure that would be much easier."

"So what are you going to do?" I was very concerned for Winston Churchill.

"I just don't know. I simply don't know," Mrs. Demir said, **squeezing all the worry out of her hands**.

"Maybe we can take him!" I offered.

"Frannie," my dad said in his stern voice.

"What?" I asked, acting as though I did not remember one single word he has ever said to me about getting a pet, which, by the way, is *No way, José.*

"We've had this discussion ten thousand times," he said.

I looked at him with my "what discussion?" look.

"About responsibility," he said, reading my mind.

"I have a real job now!" I told him. "I'm the most responsible kid in the entire world of earth!"

My dad thought for a minute. "The job's not over yet. Let's see how you fare. Then maybe we'll discuss it."

Mrs. Demir was looking back and forth between me and my dad, watching us like she was watching a tennis game. Then she saw someone pick up a quilt and she rushed over, talk-shouting, "Oh no! That's an accident! That's not for sale!"

I went back to my Lemonade Office and sat with Elliott and Winston Churchill. I patted Winston Churchill

on the head and told him not to worry.
If the Demirs couldn't take him, we'd
find a nice home for him. Elliott had
made an entire dollar while I was gone.
That was very **impresstifying**. My
dad bought an old movie projector that
had a film in it already and a suit that
belonged to Mr. Demir, and my mom
got a lot of dishware and some mother-
of-tortoiseshell hair combs. They didn't
have any kid stuff, so Elliott and I just
sold our lemonade and kept the dog out
of trouble.

When the sun started to set, we
packed up and went back to our house.
My dad set up the movie projector and
wanted to see what movie was wound
around it. He pressed play and the
movie was *My Fair Lady*! That's when
my eyeballs almost popped out of my

head with **excitification**. That is one of my favorite movies in the history of ever! My mom made popcorn and we sat in the living room and watched the movie.

"This is so perfect," my mom said, leaning back in her chair and taking a handful of popcorn.

"Completely perfect," my dad said.

"If only we had a dog," I added. "Named Winston Churchill."

Then my dad, Elliott, and my mom all leaned forward in their seats to look at me, and we burst out laughing.

CHAPTER

On Monday during gym, while I
was waiting my turn to climb the rope
ladder, a **bad day worry** dropped on
my skin. What if we never heard back
from Aimee Chapman? Or what if she
said no?! And then, what if the battle
of the bands got sick and couldn't do it,
either? Then what? And that is when I
knew exactly what! We could start our
own band and be rock stars!

I wondered how hard it actually was

to play an instrument. Maybe it was really easy, and I could learn how to play the guitar like Aimee Chapman. I ran over to Elliott, Millicent, and Elizabeth, who were all digging through the athletic bag looking for a ball.

"We need to start a band," I told them.

They all looked up, and at the same time they all said, "Okay."

"Because what if Aimee Chapman says no? Then what?" I asked.

"Battle of the bands," Elliott said.

"Or maybe just our band because we'll be so good!" I said.

"I'll be in a band," Millicent said.

"Me too!" Elliott played the clarinet, so we were already in good shape.

"I'll do it, too," Elizabeth said.

"Great! I'll see if Mrs. Glass will let

us use her music room during lunch."
Then I ran back to my spot in line for
the rope ladder.

After gym, I got permission from
Mrs. Glass and then quickly ran back
to my classroom.

I was so excited about playing an
instrument, especially because I didn't
know how to play anything. But I
worried that everyone else would want
to play the guitar and I'd have to play
something else. The tuba was good, but
it was too heavy. The piano was good,
but it seemed too **concentratey** for
me. Besides, when pianists play, you
can really only see the side of them.

I decided I would just have to run
really fast toward the guitar when
we got to the music room. I worried
all throughout reading class and all

throughout math and finally, when it was lunchtime, I ran as **fastly** as possible to the music room. But the music class hadn't even finished and I had to wait outside.

Elliott plays a lot of instruments, so I wasn't sure which one he'd want to play. But he showed up with his clarinet. Millicent came, then Elizabeth, and I was nearly sweating. Finally, the music class finished, and when the last kid walked out of the room, I ran as fast as possible to the guitar. Mrs. Glass was there and told us to treat everything with care.

"We will!" I yelled as I reached the guitar. You will not even believe your ears about this: I was the only one who wanted to play the guitar! The others ran to different instruments.

Elliott put together his clarinet, Millicent went to the piano, and Elizabeth picked up the tambourine. I put the strap around my neck and then turned to the others.

"Hey!" I said, realizing something very important. "We need a band name!"

"Oh, yeah!" everyone chimed in, very excited about this.

"How about the Elliotts?" Elliott asked.

"Or the Elizabeths?" Elizabeth asked.

"Or the Millicents?" Millicent asked.

"Well, what about me?" I asked. When everyone shrugged, I got it. "I know," I called. "The ME ME MEs!"

"Yeah!" Elliott said.

"That's a great name," Elizabeth said.

"Yeah, because it could be any one of us!" Millicent said.

"Exactly," I told them. "Now, what should the ME ME MEs play?" I asked.

We spent a really long time trying to decide this, and then when we agreed on an Aimee Chapman song, it was official. We all turned to our instruments and Elliott called out, "Ready, set, go!"

The sound we made was so terrible and so loud that my eardrums almost broke off. Everyone else had their face **squinched** up like they ate a whole lemon with the peel on. But we kept on playing our instruments, anyway. I guess we should have stopped sooner because a couple seconds into our **horrendimous song**, Cora (Principal Wilkins's assistant) and Principal Wilkins himself appeared red-faced and out of breath in the doorway.

"What is that terrible noise?"
Principal Wilkins cried.

I stopped playing first. Then
Millicent and Elizabeth. But Elliott
kept playing until he realized no one
else was playing anymore. I looked up
at Principal Wilkins.

"We're the ME ME MEs," I told him.
"We're a band."

"That was a song?" Cora asked in a
sweet voice as though she was trying to
be very polite.

"Yes. That was an Aimee Chapman
song," I told her.

"I didn't know that you even played
the guitar, Frannie," Principal Wilkins
said to me. "Or that you played the
tambourine, Elizabeth," he added. "In
fact, the only one I know for certain
plays an instrument here is Elliott!"

"We don't!" I told him.

"You don't?"

"No! But we have to be a band in case Aimee Chapman says no about playing at Noah's Ark," I explained.

"But if you don't know how to play instruments, how are you going to play those songs?"

"That's the tricky part," I told him.

"You can't just *will* yourself to play an instrument. You have to learn it first. That takes time," Principal Wilkins told us.

"That is true," Elliott said. "It took me months to learn the clarinet."

"We don't have that much time," I explained.

"I think you need a Plan B," he said.

"I agree," Cora chimed in.

"Like what?" I asked.

"Anything," Principal Wilkins said. "Anything but playing instruments."

They were probably right. We did sound terrible, and we certainly weren't naturals, which is something that I always liked to be.

"Good luck," Principal Wilkins called.

"Yeah, good luck!" Cora sang, and the two of them turned and walked back down the hall to their office.

"What should we do?" Elliott asked.

"We just have to wait," I said. It's a scientific fact that that was one of the most grown-up things I've ever said.

No one liked that answer, but we all knew it was true.

CHAPTER

After school, the three of us walked across the street to Noah's Ark. I ran up to Noah's office to hear about my next job. He was more nervous than I had ever seen him. The concert was in just five days, and we hadn't heard from Aimee Chapman.

"I'll give it until the end of the day," he told me. "Then we'll tell the local bands to get ready."

Just then, the phone rang. Noah

reached for the phone, but before he picked it up, he changed his mind.

"You get it," he told me.

I smiled and picked up the phone, saying the exact same thing Noah always did.

"Noah's Ark, how may I help you?"

The voice on the other end sounded a little bit **familiarish**.

"I'm calling to talk to Noah Zark," the voice told me.

"He's right here. Who may I say is calling, please?" I asked in my most professional voice. I was about to use my English accent, but then I decided against it. It might be weird to change my voice after someone had already heard it a little bit.

"My name is Aimee Chapman," the voice said.

That is when my skin and every inside part of me froze. I had never talked to a famous person before. Especially not an Aimee Chapman–type of famous person.

"Hello?" the voice asked.

"Uh—uh—hold on a second, okay? He is right here. Here he is. One second, please. I will give the phone to him now." I could not stop my mouth's brain from talking. Noah was looking at me strangely, and I held the phone out to him.

"Who is it?" he asked, but I could only shake my head no. I didn't know what was wrong with me. Even my head was filled with moths and butterflies.

"Hello?" Noah said, then his face turned bright red and he looked at me and smiled. I smiled right back at him.

"Wow. It's you. I can't believe it," Noah said. Then he waved me out, and I shut the door behind me and stood outside his office while he talked to the **most famous person on planet Chester**.

What felt like seventeen whole days passed by, and then suddenly the door swung open and Noah yelled, "She said yes. Aimee Chapman said yes!"

Then he grabbed my hands, and we started jumping up and down and went roundy-round in a circle like we were a merry-go-round made out of people. It was really fun. I was so, so, so **excitified** that Aimee Chapman said yes! Then Noah and I ran downstairs to tell the entire world of everyone who was at the Ark at that exact minute the very good news. Then we went right back upstairs because Aimee Chapman's manager was faxing over her rider.

Because I was Noah's assistant, he let me capture the pages as they came out of the fax's mouth. That part was really fun. I handed him the pages and watched him read. When he was done, he let me look at the rider. It looked very complicated, which made it seem very professional.

"Her green room is easy, but her stage setup is very complicated," Noah said, relieviated about the green room, but not about the other thing. But I can tell you for a scientific fact that her green room setup was *not* easy.

It was *boring*. A for instance of what I
mean is that it looked like this:

- 2 white towels
- 6 large bottles of S. Pellegrino
- A bowl of fresh, cut-up fruit.
  No kiwi
- Spearmint gum

She didn't say anything about the
walls or the couch or anything like that.
What about decorations? What about
pads and pens in case she had any
sudden brilliant brain ideas? Maybe
she would even want to make a copy
of these ideas and use a copy machine!
Maybe she didn't know about how to
decorate a room. Maybe she didn't
understand about green rooms and
how amazing they were. I knew about
green rooms, so I could tell her all about
them. Or I could just add some more

things to her rider for her. Or I could just decorate the green room the way I knew she would love it. Because I was going to be a rock star, too, I knew exactly what rock stars loved to have in their green rooms.

Noah made a phone call, and when he hung up, he told me that all the things on Aimee's rider would be delivered the morning of the show. Then I could set up her green room before she arrived. This gave me a really good idea. Setting up her room would be really fast. I would still have time to decorate it before she came!

She would be so excited to see how **amazingified** my imagination was. There would be so many cool things to play with, she'd nearly forget to give a concert because she would be

so distractified by how fun I made
her room.

When I got home, I called Elliott
and I told him all about my decorating
plan. His mom was a really decoration
type of person. She had big plastic
boxes in her basement filled with
birthday and holiday supplies. I told
him to pull some fun things from the
boxes.

In only ten minutes, Elliott called
back and said he had the **bestest**
supplies. He wanted to show me, so I
asked if he could come for dinner.

Elliott's mom, Julie, and her
boyfriend, George, dropped him off and
we ran up to my room. He unzipped
his knapsack and pulled out streamers,

a Happy New Year banner, Christmas lights, plastic sparkle glasses, and Hawaiian types of necklaces. I was very impresstified with Elliott's supplies.

I found a rolling suitcase in my parents' closet and wheeled it into my room. Then Elliott watched as I took down all my posters and rolled them up and put rubber bands around them. Then I ripped pictures of other rock stars I liked out of magazines. It was a good idea to hang up pictures of rock stars in a rock star's green room.

I had leftover Halloween candy, so I put that in the suitcase, too.

"What about some stuffed animals?" Elliott wanted to know.

I smiled my "that is a really good idea, Elliott!" smile because that was a really good idea. I put a **hundredy** stuffed animals in the suitcase. We zipped it up and rolled it over to the front door so he could take it home before bringing it back to Noah's Ark on Saturday.

CHAPTER 10

We were counting down to the big day, which was exactly one day. The Demirs were leaving two days after the concert, so before going to the Ark to help set up, my parents and I went to see how they were doing. Their house was almost empty. It was the **weirdiest** feeling to be in their house with no furniture.

"No one can take Winston Churchill," Mrs. Demir told us. "Please, I have no one else left to ask," she explained.

"Please, Mom," I begged her. "Please, please, oh pleeeeeeaaaaassssse???????"

She laughed, but looked worriedly at my dad.

"We'll discuss it, but I can't make any promises," my dad said.

Mrs. Demir reached out and hugged my dad. "Yes, please discuss it!" she said. We told her we had to leave, but would come back before they left.

"Don't forget to discuss Winston Churchill!" she called after us as we left.

When we got to the Ark, it was filled with a lot of equipment and technical-looking people. These were the people who were going to run the sound part of the concert. They were doing very interesting things with wires and big black boxes. Someone rolled a very big piano onto the stage. People rushed all around with folding chairs.

But the most incredible part was that everyone was wearing a *walkie-talkie*! I did not know that rock stars got to be around people who wore walkie-talkies! I could not believe what a great job they had. This made being a rock star even better! I wondered if the walkie-talkers had an office where they kept all the walkie-talkies. That would be a really amazing kind of office to work in.

A lot of different music stands were onstage, and Noah said the instruments would be there tomorrow for sound check. That's a technical term for rock stars that means "Let's check to see if the sound sounds good."

My job that day was an easy one: I had to clean up around the Ark. I put all the costumes away and all the toys back in the toy bin. My parents helped the technical people unfold all those chairs. When we were all done and I thought we were going to go straight home, my parents **surprisified** me!

We were going to meet Elliott, his mom, Julie, and her boyfriend, George, for dinner. At a restaurant! Elliott and I love restaurants because they are extremely fancy and professional and we get to order things that are very special, like curly fries and orange soda.

During dinner, my father and George told us that they were in a band together in college. An actual, real-life rock band. They were very good, too, is what George said.

"Not good enough to be professional," my dad said.

"Well," George said, "I thought so."

"That's because you are tone-deaf," my dad said, laughing.

"What's *tone-deaf*?" I asked.

"That's when you sing out of tune."

"And that's bad, right?" Elliott asked.

"Very," my dad answered.

"Not if your band is named the Tone-Deafs," I said.

Everyone laughed.

Because Elliott plays a lot of instruments, he has a lot of instruments in his house. After dinner, we went to Elliott's house. My dad and George said they'd play some of their old songs for us.

My dad was right: They were really terrible. But some of their songs were fun and catchy, and at the end they taught a song to us and we all sang along and it was really fun.

Then my dad let us all be in the band. I strummed the ukulele, my mom played the tambourine, Elliott played his clarinet, and Julie played the harmonica.

It was really fun, especially because it was okay that we were so terrible-sounding. Soon it was later than everyone realized, and we had to go home. I went to get ready for bed, but before I went to sleep, I had to remind my parents about something very important.

"Don't forget you are supposed to discuss taking Winston Churchill."

"We haven't forgotten," my dad said.

"Good. That is all. Good night."

"Good night, Mrs. Miller," my mom said, and they both gave me **sweet-dream** kisses.

CHAPTER

11

The next morning, Noah showed me the box where everything for Aimee Chapman's green room was. He told me to set up and he'd come look at it soon. Then he left, and I took the S. Pellegrino bottles out of the box. Soon Elliott showed up with George right behind him, wheeling the big suitcase of supplies.

Elliott and I set up the green room the way Aimee Chapman's rider said to. When we were done, Noah came and said it looked perfect. Then he turned out the light, shut the door, and told us we could do whatever we wanted until he needed us again. When he disappeared down the hall, we knew it was time to start our surprise. Noah was going to be so proud of us for thinking about decorating the green room! I might even get promoted!

We started to decorate the room. We filled it with all our toys. Then we stepped back and had a look. It looked good, but not perfect. We ran back into the main room of Noah's Ark and looked around. That's when I had a **geniusal** idea! We needed flowers and plants! We dragged one of the plant trees into the green room, and then Elliott brought in all the café-table flowers.

We took a good, long look at the beautiful work we'd done on the green room. We could hardly wait to hear Aimee Chapman tell us how much she loved what we did. Then she would add all these new things to her rider and ask for these exact decorations everywhere she went.

We turned out the lights, shut the door, and went into the theater to see if they were doing the sound check yet. A woman who was not Aimee Chapman was plunking piano keys. A man was plucking guitar strings and tapping on the microphone. He leaned over and said into it, "Microphone check, one, two, three."

It was extremely **excitifying**. I would never forget those words for the rest of my life.

Microphone check, one, two, three!

I didn't know where my parents were, but it was too exciting in there to look for them. Then the most amazing thing in the entire world happened: The man onstage, whose name was Jeff, who was playing his guitar and calling those magical words into the microphone, asked me and Elliott if we wanted to come up onstage. We could not believe our worldwide ears. *Of course* we wanted to go up onstage!

Elliott and I ran up the steps and stood next to him. He took the microphone out of its holder and spoke into it, asking me, "What's your name?"

Jeff's entire sentence filled up the whole Noah's Ark theater.

"Mrs. Frankly B. Miller," I said into the microphone. That filled up Noah's

Ark theater also. I got goose chills on my top skin.

"And yours?" he asked Elliott.

"Professor Elliott Stephenson," Elliott said.

Then Jeff told me to sit down on a chair. He put the guitar on my lap and taught me how to strum it. I was a musician! Next, he brought Elliott to the drums, gave him two sticks, and taught him how to bang on them a little bit. I felt like a real-life rock star in a real-life band, just like Aimee Chapman. It was the best feeling I'd ever had in my entire **worldwide life**.

"Thank you, Frankly," Jeff said, taking the guitar back from me.

I could hardly believe myself.

"You are very welcome, Jeff," I told him in my most **seriousal** voice. When

I looked out at the empty auditorium, I could see it filled up with a **millionty** people, cheering and clapping and calling my name. I couldn't wait to be an actual, real-life rock star and have that feeling again and again as much as I wanted.

Elliott and I ran off the stage and found everyone in Noah's office and told them about the amazing thing that had just happened.

Aimee Chapman would be there in about an hour, so we all went down the street to get sandwiches. Over sandwiches, we talked about which songs we wanted her to sing and whether she would get an encore. I thought she would get two encores, and

Elliott thought she would get three. Elliott and I could hardly believe we were going to get to meet her.

Then the **surprise of the world** came when our parents gave both Elliott and me presents. They were the exact same size and shape. We decided we would open them at the same time. When we unwrapped them, we saw they were the same book with the words AUTOGRAPH BOOK across the front. *WOW.* We'd never had autograph books before. We'd never even gotten anyone's autograph.

"Thank you!" we both said, hugging our parents.

"Aimee Chapman can be your very first autograph," my mom told me.

"And mine, too!" Elliott said.

"And yours, too!" my mom said.

We went back to Noah's Ark and changed into our fancy fund-raiser outfits. I was going to wear my most rock-starrish outfit: jeans, a white T-shirt, a very rock-star headband, and a scarf. Just like my hero, Aimee Chapman.

Then there was a big commotion and we went into the main part of Noah's Ark and saw a man walking in, talking on the phone. He was talking very loudly, and I did not like him right away. We all scrunched up our faces at how loudly he was talking.

"I'm in Chester, New York. I don't know. It's in the middle of nowhere."

Chester, New York, is not in the middle of nowhere. I did not appreciate that one bit.

"To save some rundown, little shack

in the woods. It's preposterous, but you know Aimee. She's a do-gooder."

This man was not a **truth teller**. Noah's Ark was not a shack! Finally, he got off the phone and looked at us.

"Who are you?" he asked.

We looked at one another a little **stumpified**.

Then my dad took a step toward him and said, "Hi, I'm Dan Miller."

"Great. Get me a coffee. Black. No sugar."

"I'm sorry, I don't actually work here," my dad said.

Then the man turned to my mom and said, "Coffee. Black. No sugar."

"I don't work here, either," my mom said.

That's when I realized that making coffee was part of my job description!

"I'll make your coffee," I said. My parents looked at me, **surprisified**.

"Coffee. Black. No sugar," he said.

"Okay," I told him. "I'll be right back."

Even if you don't like someone, you have to do your job. I went into the kitchen and found the coffeemaker. I couldn't exactly remember the instructions. I knew I had to pour water and coffee into the coffeemaker and then press the on button. I scooped out the coffee, but wasn't sure where to dump it. I decided to put it in the pitcher thing and filled it with water. Then I pressed the on button.

I went back to where the mean man

was and said, "It shouldn't take long."

My dad politely excused himself and went toward the kitchen, and my mom and I played a game of jacks while we waited for Aimee Chapman to show up. Soon I could smell coffee. I couldn't believe how good it smelled. I did it! **I actually made coffee!** I ran into the kitchen and my dad was standing next to the machine, pouring a cup of coffee.

"I can't believe it worked!" I said.

"Actually, it didn't. I made this. We'll go over the instructions again at home."

"Oh," I said, disappointed.

"But you were close," he said, smiling at me. That made me feel better.

We could hear the mean man yelling for his coffee. He was really not a nice person. I certainly hoped Aimee Chapman was nicer than him. Just then, we heard the mean man's voice again, only this time it was much nicer.

"There she is!" he shouted. "Aimee, great to see you."

My dad and I left the kitchen and saw my actual favorite rock star on this earth: Aimee Chapman. Noah came downstairs to meet her, and when he introduced me I got very **shy-ish**.

"I got your letter," she told me.

"You did?"

"Yes, and I loved it. It convinced me that I should come help out. Thanks for sending it, Frankly," Aimee Chapman said to me.

I nearly fell over with happiness. But I didn't. I stayed standing up, because there was still a lot left to do.

CHAPTER 12

Noah pointed Aimee Chapman toward the green room and went to check on the auditorium. Soon people started to show up, and there was a lot of excitement in the air. The seats were filling up fast. Soon there were no more seats left and people were standing. It was almost time to get Aimee.

Noah went to tell her she was going on in five minutes, but when he came back, his face was **not a good color**.

"She's gone!" he said.

"What do you mean *gone*?" my mom asked.

"She's not in the green room—which looks very different from the rider, by the way." He said that last part looking at me.

I squinched up my face at that sentence.

"Did you look all over the place?"

"Not yet. Help me look."

We all split up and looked absolutely everywhere. We checked every single room, but she was nowhere to be found. Not even in the bathroom. Her manager was outside yelling on his phone. Noah went to get him. That is when I got a very **sinking** feeling in my guts. What if she changed her mind and left? What were we going to do? I would be very responsible for all of it. Aimee Chapman was my idea in the first place. Also, I had a **real-life job** at the Ark, which meant I had to solve Ark problems!

I had to figure out what to do if we never found her. I would have to save the day. If I didn't save the day, then people would think I wasn't responsible. And if they thought that I wasn't responsible, I'd never get another job again. And also, I would never be allowed to have a dog. Especially one named Winston Churchill.

Aimee's manager came inside and tried calling her, but it just went straight to her voice mail. Noah was pacing back and forth worrying his brain off. Even her manager looked very nervous, indeed.

"I'll be right back," I said, and ran to the auditorium. Maybe she was there! The auditorium was completely overflowing with people. The technical instrument people were waiting on the side in their professional, black concert clothes. Music was playing over the loudspeaker, and everyone was so **excitified**, they could barely keep their brains inside their heads. But Aimee Chapman was not there.

And that is when I realized right then and there what I needed to do. Aimee Chapman had changed her mind and gone home. I was going to have to save the day.

I walked up the three little steps to the stage. I had the biggest moths and butterflies in my belly. I was about to be a rock star. I couldn't believe how

exciting and **nervousing** that felt.
I walked to the center of the stage,
and a big, hot spotlight shined on me.
Everyone quieted down, which made
me feel very important, indeed. When I
looked out into the audience, everyone
was dark, like paper cutout dolls. I
couldn't see anyone, and I had to hold
my hand over my eyes like a visor. The
microphone was very high up, and I
bent it down as low as it would go.

"Hello, everyone," I said into the
microphone. My voice was so loud, it
flooded the entire room.

"Hi!" everyone yelled back at me.
Wow. I had the entire town of Chester's
attention. This was the best feeling in
the **entire worldwide of America**.

"I have good news and bad news,"
I said. This is a for instance of

something my dad always says. He says to always start with the bad news. If the good news is second, then people will walk away happy!

"The bad news is that Aimee Chapman had to go home. I don't know why, but she just did—" Before I could continue on to the good news, people started to get really upset. There was a lot of commotion. People were talking and making noises like they were very upset about this news. A couple of people walked out. I really did not like the bad part of this moment. I had to make the good part come right away.

"But the good news is that I am going to play for you," I said into the microphone. "I know all of Aimee's songs."

But people were so loud that

no one could even hear me.

I ran over to the guitar, but when I tried to pick it up, it was too heavy for me. So I sat down on a chair and laid the guitar on my lap.

I started to strum it, and the worst, **most terrible** sounds came out of the guitar. That's when I thought I should start singing to drown out the terrible noise of the guitar. So that's what I started to do, but since I wasn't singing in the microphone, no one could hear.

I decided to leave the guitar and go sing into the microphone so everyone could hear me.

I do not have the best voice in the entire world of America, but it's not the *worst* voice, either. **Apparently and nevertheless**, the audience did not seem to love it.

But I kept going because I knew that I had to sing at least one entire song. Halfway through the song, the audience decided that they actually really loved me because they started clapping and whooping and standing up. I smiled really **bigly** and sang louder. Wow, being a rock star really was the best feeling in the world.

But then I heard something that hadn't been there before—a guitar! I turned around and there, standing right off to the side, was Aimee Chapman! The guitar I had just been playing was strapped around her and she was playing perfectly. She walked over to the microphone where I was standing.

"You didn't leave!" I said into the microphone.

"Of course I didn't leave!" she said. "Why would I do that?"

"You weren't in the green room," I told her.

"Oh, it was too cluttered!" she said. "I went upstairs. To Noah's office. Plus, there were flowers in the green room, and I'm very allergic."

Whoops.

"I think that was my fault," I admitted.

"We can talk about that later. First, don't you think we should sing a song?" she asked me.

The entire audience went **berserk**, and I got the rock-star feeling I'd always dreamed about. Aimee lowered a microphone to my level and told me to sing along with her onstage! She played the song I had been playing when she

came onstage, but she was much better at it than I was. I didn't sing as loud because I felt shy, but I did sing, and it was the most **amazingish** feeling. When the song was done, we got a standing ovation! I bowed and then I went into the audience and took my seat next to my parents, who gave me a look that said "we are sort of proud of you, but also you are in trouble."

The concert was actually amazing, and when it was all over, my parents and I went to find Aimee Chapman. My parents wanted me to apologize for putting so many things in her green room when she had only asked for a few boring things. And also to say I was very sorry about the flowers. I thought I was giving her a surprise that she would love, but actually I gave her a surprise that she hated.

"That's what riders are for," she explained to me after the concert.

"I thought you didn't know you were allowed to decorate the room, too!" I told her.

"Oh, I know all about that. I've been doing this a very long time. It's always good to know what you need and it's always good to ask for it, but you know what's even better than that?" she asked me.

"No, what?" I asked her.

"When people listen to my needs and wants."

I gulped hard.

"I'm sorry, Aimee. I didn't think of it like that," I told her.

"I know you didn't, but you need to from now on. Being a rock star looks like a lot of fun, and it is, but it's serious business, too. I do things a certain way so that I can play a good show for everyone. The more calm I am before I go onstage, the better."

"That makes sense," I told her.

"Good," she said. "So from now on, when adults tell you what they want, are you going to listen?" she asked.

"I'm sure going to try!" I said.

"That's good enough for me," she said.

"Aimee?" I said as we walked down the hall toward her calm green room.

"Yes, Frankly?"

"I'm sorry I ruined your life," I said.

"Oh, Frankly. You did no such thing!" Then she put her arm around my shoulder and I almost **fell over from happiness**.

Her mean manager came over to us and he was yelling on the phone. Aimee gestured for him to get off, but he turned his back and ignored her.

"Chris," she said to him, "please get off the phone. This is a fund-raiser. I really don't think you should be doing business now."

He looked very irritated and walked outside and kept talking on the phone.

Aimee looked at me and said, "Frankly, if you don't start listening to people, you will grow up and be like my manager. And you know what happens to grown-ups who don't listen?"

I shook my head.

"They get fired from jobs."

That's when I gasped in a breath of "I do not want that to ever happen to me" air.

But it also reminded me of something.

"Don't go anywhere," I told her. "I have something for you!"

Then I ran into the green room where I had put my bag. I pulled out the manila envelope with my résumé and rider in it. I ran back to Aimee and handed it to her.

"What is this?" she asked me.

"That's my résumé. Just in case you ever need to hire me," I said.

She laughed really hard, but not at me, which was good. Then she said, "Frankly, I'm so glad I met you."

I felt the exact same way.

"Now, if you'll excuse me, I have to go fire my manager."

ice-cream flavor. Then he went to the
ice-cream counter and scooped some
Frankly Franberry into a cone and
handed it to me.

As I licked my flavor-named ice
cream, I thought I couldn't get one inch
happier. But I was wrong.

My parents walked over to me and I gave them each a lick.

"You know who I bet would love that ice cream?" my mom asked me.

"Who?" I wanted to know, thinking she'd say Elliott.

"Your new dog," my dad said.

I gasped out loud. "Winston Churchill?!"

"Winston Churchill," my mom said.

"We decided to give you a chance. If you can't be responsible for a pet, we'll give him to someone who can be. Understand?"

I nodded. Then I ran to tell Elliott, who couldn't believe his **worldwide ears** about this news.

I was going to add the word *Doctor* in front of my dog's name. That sounded much more professional than just

Winston Churchill. Doctor Winston Churchill. I could not wait!

Before the party ended, Elliott and I ran to our bags and brought Aimee Chapman our autograph books. She wrote:

> Dear Frankly,
> I'm so glad I met you. Don't forget to listen to others, and in return, they will listen to you.
> With love, Aimee Chapman

That was when I knew I actually could not get one inch happier than I already was.

THE END.

Want more Frannie?

Check Out All the Books in the Series Including

Frankly Frannie: Here Comes the . . . Trouble
Coming Soon!

Frannie has the important job of flower girl in Elliott's mother's wedding a
Frannie discovers her latest calling: Wedding Planner! Frannie and Elliot
work together to make sure his mother has the best wedding day ever, bu
with Frannie involved, you can count on some wedding day mayhem.

Visit FranklyFrannie.com

- Make your own business cards and résumé
- Write a very official letter
- Make your own sock doll
- Take a quiz to find out your perfect job
- Read all about Frannie's books
  ...and more!

If you have a job offer for Frannie, please call 212-414-3745